Sinbad and the Monkeys

by Jackie Walter and Simone Fumagalli

W

FRANKLIN WATTS
LONDON•SYDNEY

Long ago, in the city of Baghdad, there lived a sailor called Sinbad. Sinbad sailed to sea and had many adventures. He made lots of money.

Sinbad was a kind man. Whenever he came home from his adventures, he shared his money with the poorest people.

Once, on the way home from an adventure, Sinbad's ship was attacked by some enormous birds. The ship sank, and Sinbad and the sailors were thrown into the sea.

Sinbad grabbed a piece of wood and held on
tight until he was washed up on an island.
He scrambled onto the rocky shore and
lay down to rest.

When he woke up, Sinbad started to look for food and water. There were coconuts high up in some tall trees, but Sinbad didn't know how to reach them.

He watched as some monkeys climbed up
to the top of the trees to eat the coconuts.
But when Sinbad went near the trees,
the monkeys screeched angrily at him.

Sinbad was afraid, and he ran quickly back to the rocky shore.

"I'm so hungry, but I'll never be able to reach the coconuts," thought Sinbad. "Those monkeys are too dangerous. I cannot stay here, but how can I get back to Baghdad?"

Just then, Sinbad spotted a ship sailing nearby.

He waved and shouted as loud as he could.

The ship's captain saw him and sent

a rowing boat ashore.

"Ahoy!" Sinbad shouted to the sailors.

"Ahoy!" came the reply. "Do you want to come back to our ship?"

"Yes please," said Sinbad.

"Then we will take you," said the sailors.

"But first, we have work to do."

The sailors climbed out of the boat, carrying

huge, empty sacks. They began to collect

lots of stones from the shore.

The sailors told Sinbad that they had come to the island to collect coconuts.

Sinbad followed the sailors to the tall trees. He did not know how they could reach the coconuts. He was sure the monkeys would attack.

Then the sailors began throwing the stones they had collected up at the monkeys.

"Stop!" cried Sinbad in horror. "If you attack them, they will attack us!"

And the monkeys did attack. They screeched and began to pick lots of coconuts from high in the trees. They threw the hard coconuts at the sailors far below.

Quickly, Sinbad and the sailors ran and hid behind some bushes. The monkeys were angry and kept throwing coconuts. Soon, the ground was covered with coconuts.

When there were no coconuts left to throw, the monkeys left the trees.

Sinbad and the sailors came out from behind the bushes and filled the empty sacks with the coconuts.

"We could sell these coconuts for a good price in Baghdad," said Sinbad with a smile.

"Then we should go to Baghdad!" cried one of the sailors.

Everyone agreed.

17

Sinbad and the sailors rowed back
to the ship with sacks full of coconuts.
What an exciting adventure
Sinbad would have to tell
when he got back to Baghdad!

Story order

Look at these 5 pictures and captions.
Put the pictures in the right order
to retell the story.

1

The sailors threw stones at the monkeys.

2

Sinbad washed up on an island.

3

Sinbad's ship was sunk by the birds.

4

Sinbad and the sailors collected the coconuts.

5

The monkeys threw coconuts at the sailors.

Independent Reading

This series is designed to provide an opportunity for your child to read on their own. These notes are written for you to help your child choose a book and to read it independently.

In school, your child's teacher will often be using reading books which have been banded to support the process of learning to read. Use the book band colour your child is reading in school to help you make a good choice. *Sinbad and the Monkeys* is a good choice for children reading at White Band in their classroom to read independently.

The aim of independent reading is to read this book with ease, so that your child enjoys the story and relates it to their own experiences.

About the book

This is an Arabic tale in which Sinbad's ship is wrecked, and he is washed up on an island where some very angry monkeys live.

Before reading

Help your child to learn how to make good choices by asking:
"Why did you choose this book? Why do you think you will enjoy it?"
Ask your child whether they have heard any other stories about Sinbad. Then look at the cover with your child and ask: "Do you think the monkeys in this story will be friendly to Sinbad?"
Remind your child that they can break words into groups of syllables or sound out letters to make a word if they get stuck.
Decide together whether your child will read the story independently or read it aloud to you.

During reading

Remind your child of what they know and what they can do independently. If reading aloud, support your child if they hesitate or ask for help by telling them the word. If reading to themselves, remind your child that they can come and ask for your help if stuck.

After reading

Support comprehension by asking your child to tell you about the story. Use the story order puzzle to encourage your child to retell the story in the right sequence, in their own words. The correct sequence can be found on the next page.

Help your child think about the messages in the book that go beyond the story and ask: "What kind of person do you think Sinbad is? Do you think he is good at facing different situations?"

Give your child a chance to respond to the story: "What was your favourite part? What did you think would happen when the sailors threw the stones at the monkeys?"

Extending learning

Help your child predict other possible outcomes of the story by asking: "What would have happened if the ship had not arrived? Would Sinbad have escaped in a different way? Would he have made friends with the monkeys?"

In the classroom, your child's teacher may be teaching recognition of recurring literary language in stories and traditional tales, and different sentence openers. The story contains examples you can look at together such as:

"Long ago", "Once", "Just then", "When".

Find these examples in the story. Think about how they help to structure the story and are often used to begin or end sentences.

Franklin Watts
First published in Great Britain in 2022
by Hodder and Stoughton

Copyright © Hodder and Stoughton Ltd, 2022

Series Editors: Jackie Hamley and Melanie Palmer
Series Advisors and Development Editors: Dr Sue Bodman and Glen Franklin
Series Designers: Peter Scoulding and Cathryn Gilbert

A CIP catalogue record for this book is
available from the British Library.

ISBN 978 1 4451 8441 8 (hbk)
ISBN 978 1 4451 8442 5 (pbk)
ISBN 978 1 4451 8522 4 (library ebook)
ISBN 978 1 4451 8523 1 (ebook)

Printed in China

Franklin Watts
An imprint of
Hachette Children's Group
Part of Hodder and Stoughton
Carmelite House
50 Victoria Embankment
London EC4Y 0DZ

An Hachette UK Company
www.hachette.co.uk

www.reading-champion.co.uk

Answer to Story order: 3, 2, 1, 5, 4